Howard and Gracie's Luncheonette

BY STEVEN KROLL   ILLUSTRATED BY MICHAEL SOURS

HENRY HOLT AND COMPANY   NEW YORK

For Abigail
—S.K.

Text copyright © 1991 by Steven Kroll
Illustrations copyright © 1991 by Michael Sours
All rights reserved, including the right to reproduce
this book or portions thereof in any form.
Published by Henry Holt and Company, Inc.,
115 West 18th Street, New York, New York 10011.
Published in Canada by Fitzhenry & Whiteside Limited,
195 Allstate Parkway, Markham, Ontario L3R 4T8.

Library of Congress Cataloging-in-Publication Data
Kroll, Steven.
   Howard and Gracie's luncheonette / by Steven Kroll;
pictures by Michael Sours.
   Summary: Depicts a typical day, from opening, through breakfast,
lunch, and dinner, to closing, of a busy luncheonette.
   ISBN 0-8050-1305-9 (alk. paper)
   [1. Restaurants, lunch rooms, etc.—Fiction.]
I. Sours, Michael, ill.   II. Title.
PZ7.K9225Hr   1991
[E]—dc20   90-40937

Henry Holt books are available at special discounts
for bulk purchases for sales promotions, premiums,
fund-raising, or educational use. Special editions
or book excerpts can also be created to specification.

First Edition

Printed in the United States of America
on acid-free paper. ∞

10 9 8 7 6 5 4 3 2 1

It's early in the morning and still dark. Howard and Gracie arrive at their luncheonette. Howard opens the door with his key.

There are the racks with the magazines and newspapers and the candy stand near the cash register. There is the counter with the polished top and the red menus standing along it.

There are the ten shiny red stools in front of the counter and the two wooden booths in the back. "It always looks so pretty," Gracie says.

A moment later, Big Joe arrives with the daily papers. He tosses them in front of the door, waves to Howard and Gracie, and speeds off in his truck. Howard carries in the papers and sets them on the rack.

Gracie is polishing the soda fountain when Chuck delivers two big containers of chocolate syrup. He hoists them onto the counter.

"Looks like a nice day coming," says Chuck.

"Sure does," says Gracie. "Thanks, Chuck."

After that, Harry delivers ten dozen fresh eggs, and Gracie begins making tuna-fish, chicken, and egg salads and slicing down the ham and the turkey she cooked last night. Everything fits neatly into the stainless-steel containers behind the counter.

Meanwhile, Howard is in back baking two apple pies, one lemon meringue, two blueberry, and two coconut custard. He is also baking a chocolate cake and muffins and many loaves of bread.

The sun comes up. Pete the cook arrives and ties on his apron. The day is ready to begin.

The bell over the door tinkles as the first customers arrive. They are Bob and Ed, two truck drivers who stop by every morning for breakfast.

"Hi," says Gracie. "What'll it be?"

"The usual," Bob replies.

"Pete," says Gracie, "flapjacks and sausage and two eggs over easy
with a side of whiskey down. Two coffees, one black, one regular no
sugar."

Pete gets to work. Out come two soft, turned-over eggs with rye toast. Out come one black coffee and one coffee with milk but no sugar. Then it's time to flip the pancakes.

"Bet you can't flip 'em three times over in the air," says Ed.
"Place your bets," says Pete.
Up go the pancakes, one after the other, soaring end over end and landing back on the griddle with a pop and a sizzle.

As Bob and Ed are finishing, Henrietta comes in for her corn muffin and coffee. Henrietta teaches third grade at the school down the road.

As Gracie brings the muffin, she says, "Henrietta, I always wonder why you come in so early. School doesn't start for another hour."

"I like being early," Henrietta says, and smiles.

Howard has been placing the fresh cake and pies in the case behind the counter. As he finishes, Fred, the local policeman, stops in for coffee.

"Mmm," he says. "If I weren't on a diet, I'd have some of that custard pie right now."

"I know about your willpower," says Gracie. She saves him a piece for later.

It's getting close to rush hour, and suddenly the little luncheonette is crowded with people. Howard is busy filling take-out orders for coffee and tea and muffins.

Gracie is serving a full counter and the booths besides. Pete is doing wonders at the grill.

When everyone has gone and the rush hour is over, Gracie plops down on a stool. "Whew," she says. "Every day, that wears me out."

Howard puts his arm around her. "But every day, you do such a job."

"And every day, you get a free cup of coffee," says Pete, pushing one across the counter.

Gracie sighs and smiles. Then she drinks her coffee.
In the blink of an eye, people start coming in for early lunch. A well-dressed woman orders fruit salad and cottage cheese. A young man buries his head in a book as he devours a ham sandwich.

Then Dr. Sanders appears.

"Hi, Doc," says Gracie, wiping the counter.

"Hello, Gracie," says the doctor, wiping his glasses. "I'd like a vanilla milkshake and a piece of Howard's chocolate cake, please."

"That's not a very healthy lunch, Doc," says Gracie.

Dr. Sanders laughs. "You won't tell my patients, will you?"

And then it is time for the lunch crowd. Pete is grilling hamburgers and making sandwiches as fast as he can. Gracie is balancing plates of food on each arm.

Howard is standing at the register, ringing up sales one after the other.

When old Professor Hotchkiss comes in to buy a newspaper, Howard hardly has time to say hello.

"You know," says the professor, "this is a very friendly place."

Howard rings up another sale.

"Except at lunchtime," says the professor.

Howard looks apologetic. "We try," he says.

Professor Hotchkiss marches out the door.

Then he comes back in and smiles. "You're right," he says. "I wish I had time to stay."

But now there's a fuss at the counter. Andy Bender has spilled his Coke. Gracie mops up the mess, and Pete fixes another Coke for Andy.

When the lunch crowd has gone, it is almost time for the after-school crowd. Soon kids are running in and out, buying gum and candy.

A bunch of teenagers takes over the booths and orders ice-cream sodas and milkshakes.

They stay for a while, eating and laughing. Then two boys start throwing straws. "All right," says Pete, "enough of that." He leads them outside. Before very long, the others follow.

Gracie sighs in relief. "Thanks, Pete."

Pete bows low. "For you, Gracie, almost anything."

Gracie laughs and curtsies back.

For a little while there is very little business. Fred the policeman returns for his piece of custard pie. A man comes in for a magazine, and Joanne from around the corner hops up on a stool and says, "I want a triple-scoop chocolate cone."

"How will you carry it?" Pete asks.

"Straight to my mouth," says Joanne.

Then the customers begin arriving for early dinner. Mostly they are older people by themselves.

Ancient Mrs. Dorinsky appears and orders a hot turkey sandwich. And in comes Jenny Donovan with her dust-mop dog, Kelly. No dogs are allowed in the luncheonette, but Gracie makes an exception for Kelly.

Jenny Donovan orders fish cakes and spaghetti.

"How can you eat that stuff?" says Mrs. Dorinsky.
"You should try it," says Jenny Donovan, and a conversation begins.
When the two have finished eating, they leave together.
"Why don't we go to a movie?" says Mrs. Dorinsky.
"What a good idea," says Jenny Donovan.
Howard, Gracie, and Pete look at each other and smile.

By then it is dark and getting late. Pete helps Howard and Gracie clean up, takes off his apron, and leaves.

Howard and Gracie make sure everything is ready for tomorrow and put on their coats.

As he locks the door behind him, Howard says, "You know, Gracie, I love this place."

"I love it too," says Gracie.